DOUNE PRIMARY SCHOOL

KU-711-781

Kingfisher Books, Grisewood & Dempsey Ltd,
Elsley House, 24-30 Great Titchfield Street,
London W1P 7AD

First published in 1993 by Kingfisher Books
2 4 6 8 10 9 7 5 3 1

Material in this edition was previously published by
Kingfisher Books in *Animal Life Stories: The Elephant*
in 1989.

Series editor: Veronica Pennycook
Series designer: Terry Woodley
Cover illustration by Doreen McGuinness/Garden Studio
Typeset in 3B2
Phototypeset by SPAN
Printed in Great Britain by
BPCC Paulton Books Limited

The Elephant

Angela Royston
Illustrated by Bob Bampton

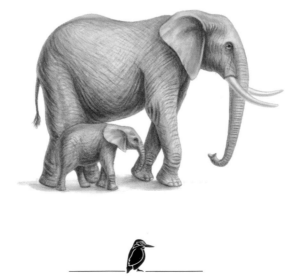

Kingfisher Books

In this book

The elephants in this story are African elephants. They live on the grassy plains of Central and Southern Africa.

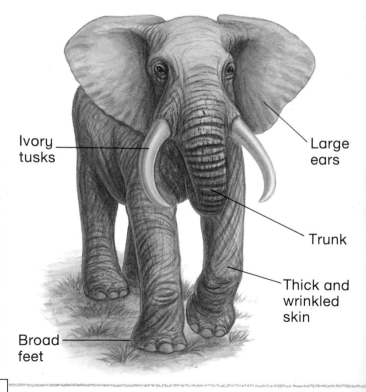

Ivory tusks

Large ears

Trunk

Thick and wrinkled skin

Broad feet

The only other type of elephant that is still alive today is the Asiatic elephant. These elephants live in the jungles of India and Southeast Asia. African elephants have much bigger ears than Asiatic elephants.

African elephant

Asiatic elephant

Looking for water

It has not rained for nearly three months. The plain is dusty and all the elephants are thirsty.

The mother elephant can smell water nearby, even though she can't see any. She plods off to find it, with her two calves behind her. The rest of the herd follow.

Just over a low hill, the elephants reach a waterhole. A few zebras and gazelles are already gathered around it.

When they hear the heavy tread of the elephants, the other animals run off. They'll wait until the elephants have finished at the waterhole.

Splash!

The leader of the herd drinks first, then the mother elephant. She sucks the cool water up into her trunk before spraying it over her back. Then she lies down so the water flows over her itchy skin.

Her bull calf wades into the pool, squealing with delight. His younger four-year-old sister

splashes in after him. When
they've had enough to drink they
play together, squirting each other
with water and rolling over to
wallow in the mud.

Waiting for the rain

Three weeks later the elephants are still waiting for the rains to come. The grass is dry and there is very little food.

They knock over trees so they can reach the highest leaves and rip the bark off the baobab trees.

At last huge dark rain clouds begin to gather over the hills. The mother elephant sniffs the air and trumpets loudly as the first drops of rain fall. The dry waterholes and river-beds will soon be full of water again.

The bull elephant

The rain falls every day. As the elephants wander over the plains eating the fresh green grass, two bull elephants follow them.

The two elephants often wrestle together, pushing each other with their trunks to find out which of them is stronger.

One evening the stronger bull elephant lumbers over to the mother. He comes close to her and they touch each other with their trunks. He knows she is ready to mate now.

When they have mated the bull wanders off and the mother goes back to the herd.

Digging for water

After many weeks the rains stop suddenly. The hot sun is beating down again, so the elephants shelter under trees. White egrets eat the insects that bother them.

The calves are thirsty, so the mother elephant takes them to a waterhole she knows. It has dried up already but she can smell water under the surface.

She digs a hole with her tusks. As the calves watch, it slowly fills up with water.

A new calf

The seasons pass. For nearly two years a calf grows inside the mother. When it's time for the calf to be born she plods away to a secret place with two older females to help her. As soon as he is born, the new calf tries to stand up, but his knees are wobbly.

He flops down. The elephants nudge him with their trunks and tusks. They push him up again and again until he is strong enough to stand and suck his mother's milk.

Two days later the new calf can join the herd as it moves on.

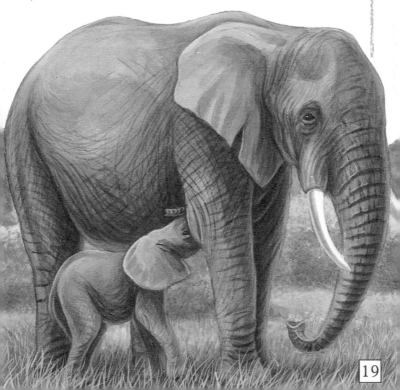

Danger

The baby elephant grows quickly, and is soon learning to look for food for himself.

One day he is grazing on his own when a hungry lioness creeps silently towards him. The egrets sense danger and fly away in alarm. The mother elephant looks to see what has alarmed the birds. She sees the lioness immediately.

The lioness snarls. The mother elephant trumpets fiercely before lowering her head and charging. Frightened of her tusks, the lioness moves away.

After this, the baby elephant is not so keen to wander away from his mother when they are feeding. He feels much safer when he stays close to her.

The broken tusk

The baby elephant grows bigger and stronger. He likes to play with the other young elephants. But his mother keeps him away from his rough older brother.

One day his brother charges at his sister. She gets a bad cut and one of her tusks is broken.

The young bull elephant is thirteen years old now and it is time for him to leave the herd. The older cow elephants bang into him and push him away.

On his own

Although the bull elephant squeals to his mother for help, she ignores him. His family walk away, but the elephant is not on his own for long. He joins a small herd of bull elephants.

The young female calf stays with the herd. She helps to look after the baby elephant, making sure he is not left behind. In another five or six years she will be old enough to mate and have a calf of her own.

Some special words

Baobab trees These have a woody pulp inside. When plants and water are scarce, elephants will rip off the bark and chew the pulp.

Bull Male elephant.

Calf Young elephant.

Cow Female elephant.

Egrets These birds eat the insects that bother elephants. When danger comes the egrets fly up in a panic.

Gazelle A kind of small deer.

Waterhole A pool or lake where animals come to drink.

Index